CW01086084

'Twas the Day of Christmas by Johnny Marfia
Join Marco, Pet Pom Dog and Santa for the Holidays

Illustrated by Jeffery Brooks

Published by Marco & Me Publishing
Part of the Marco & Me Books

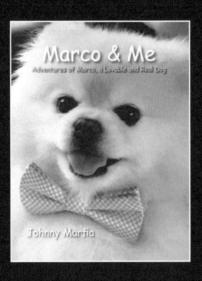

Printed in the United States of America

First Edition

ISBN: 979-8-9895153-0-1 (paperback)

ISBN: 979-8-9895153-1-8 (eBook)

'Twas the Day of Christmas

About the Author

Inducted into two Halls of Fame, a former teacher and head coach, Johnny Marfia is now the author of 'Twas the Day of Christmas. He recently became recognized as an award-winning author for his first published book, *Marco & Me: Adventures of Marco, a Lovable and Real Dog* by the American Book Fest – American Fiction Award in Juvenile Fiction and notably, he also received an official rating of 5 stars from Readers' Favorite. Marco & Me, has been read and used in elementary schools, community youth centers, libraries and book festivals.

Marco, a loving Pomeranian, motivated John to become a children's author to share positivity with young readers through Marco's photos and his short stories. Marco has brought an unparalleled appreciation for the simple joys in life, and his brightness shines strong amidst unsettling times.

John is hoping that his holiday book, 'Twas the Day of Christmas, will bring smiles and enjoyment to children of all ages while reading about Marco's playful journey on Christmas Day.

This children's book is dedicated to Marco's veterinarians, who are nothing short of miraculous. Without them, there may not have been any children's book to write or story to tell. A world of gratitude for their compassion, dedication, exceptional medical expertise and tender loving care to our boy Marco.

Tim Mosebey, VMD

Dominique Sawyere, BVSc, MS, DACVS(SA)

Guy DeNardo, DVM

'Twas the day of Christmas, when all through our home,

Our dog named MARCO was
just starting out to roam.

He was envisioning Santa with his
reindeer flying through the sky,
And now Marco was wondering if
Santa had stopped by.

From the bedroom he ran
as quick as can be,
While visions of treats he
was hoping to see!

Down the steps to the kitchen
he went,
Marco was focused and running
with intent!

He put his head down
and nose to the floor;
Using his senses,
Marco was smelling
and looking with
much to explore.

But Marco found not even a crumb,
So he continued his search in hopes of
finding some.

Around and around he
checked the kitchen out,

But nothing came about,
and Marco started to pout.

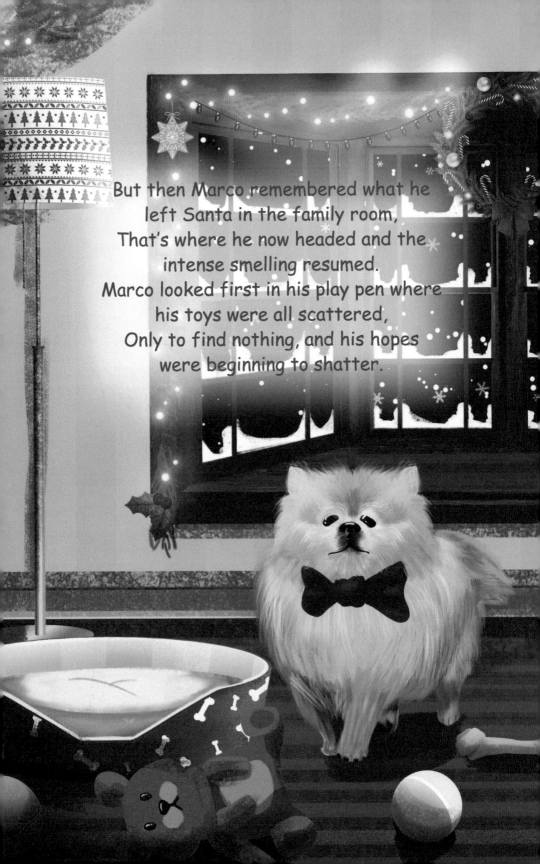

But then Marco remembered what he
left Santa in the family room,
That's where he now headed and the
intense smelling resumed.
Marco looked first in his play pen where
his toys were all scattered,
Only to find nothing, and his hopes
were beginning to shatter.

He thought for a moment and then
pranced toward the fireplace;
Marco realized the fire was out and only
ashes were left in its place.
Marco sat there for a while with a sad
look on his face;
He was disappointed in Santa having not
left a trace.

But then, random thoughts flashed through Marco's mind,
If Santa were here, then he knew what would not have been left behind.
So Marco dashed over to the wooden stool by the Christmas tree,
He was hoping to see any little sign that Santa was not an absentee.

Much to Marco's delight, Santa's cookies
and milk were gone;
He now knew that Santa had been there
before dawn!

Marco sniffed and sniffed until his senses honed in; He knew he was getting closer to where Santa had been.

And then, in a gigantic smile,
and with a titled head,
Marco began barking at the
mantle that was overhead.

He didn't stop barking until his
stocking was taken down;
He then pushed his nose inside
and was going to town!

Marco was so happy that Santa
remembered the family pet;
Just like kids, Marco got his
wish and now he is all set.

So Marco has one last wish for
all of you today,

"MERRY CHRISTMAS TO ALL,
AND TO ALL A GREAT DAY!"

Printed in Great Britain
by Amazon

55831670R00021